For Thomas, Lupita, and for you —B. G. L.

Copyright © 2002 by Atlantis, an imprint of Orell Füssli Verlag AG,
Zürich, Switzerland
First published in Switzerland under the title *Flieg, Flengel flieg!*
English translation copyright © 2005 by North-South Books Inc., New York

First published in the United States, Great Britain, Canada, Australia, and New Zealand in 2005 by North-South Books, an imprint of NordSüd Verlag AG, Gossau Zürich, Switzerland.

Distributed in the United States by North-South Books Inc., New York.
Library of Congress Cataloging-in-Publication Data is available.
A CIP catalogue record for this book is available from The British Library.
ISBN 0-7358-2024-4 (trade edition) 10 9 8 7 6 5 4 3 2 1
ISBN 0-7358-2025-2 (library edition) 10 9 8 7 6 5 4 3 2 1

Printed in Belgium

Dreamflight

Brigitta Garcia López

Photographs by Felix Streuli
Translated by Marianne Martens

North-South Books
New York/London

EEEEEEK! Max's mother let out a piercing scream and raced around the house in terror.

It all began one summer day when Mother went to put on her left shoe. Something was jammed into the toe, so her foot wouldn't fit. She peered suspiciously inside the shoe. Two shiny eyes peered back at her. She froze. At first, she was ready to throw her shoe away. Instead, she turned it upside down and gave it a good shake.

SPLAT! Something fell to the floor. Before Max's mother could see what it was, it flew off. That was when she screamed. She chased after the mysterious flying object, but soon lost sight of it. She ran through the house, searching everywhere for the flying monster, but she couldn't find it anywhere. Whatever it was had settled in Max's room, where it hid and took a long nap.

That night, Max was awakened by what sounded like the roar of an engine. Shocked, he snapped on his bedside lamp. He couldn't believe his eyes! His little red racing car was speeding through the room at breakneck speed. Behind the wheel was a little man who seemed to be having a terrific time. When the little man noticed that Max was watching him, he parked the car beside Max's bed. Chuckling, he spread his wings and flew right up in front of Max's nose.

"Hi there! I'm Wilbur, and I'm your guardian angel.
I've been following you everywhere ever since you
were born but you couldn't see me until now."
Max had no idea what this Wilbur was talking about.
"Am I awake, or am I dreaming?"
"You are wide awake," shouted Wilbur, pinching
Max's ear.

"Yeow!"

"Hey not so loud—otherwise you'll wake your mother."

"You know my mother?"

"In a way," said Wilbur.

Wilbur flew excitedly around the room and told Max all about his little encounter with Max's mother—and about her bloodcurdling scream.

Finally he landed on a piece of chocolate on a shelf, which he began to gobble up greedily. "Mmmm, your chocolate is certainly delicious!"

"What is a guardian angel anyway?" asked Max.

"Don't you know that every child has his own guardian angel?" Wilbur couldn't believe Max's ignorance. He sighed. "I guess hardly anyone knows. And yet we accompany you everywhere, day and night. It's really hard work, let me tell you. Usually we're invisible, but I thought since you just moved here and seemed so lonely and bored that I would make myself visible to cheer you up."

Wilbur quickly bit off another chunk of chocolate.

Max must have dozed off again, for the next thing he knew the sun was shining in the window. He sat up in bed and rubbed his eyes. Had he been dreaming? Where was Wilbur? Max looked around his room. Nothing was moving. He concentrated hard. He was quite sure he hadn't been dreaming. Quietly, he whispered Wilbur's name. Nothing. He called a little louder. "Wilbur, are you there?" But there was no answer. He snuggled back under the covers.

"Good morning Max! Did you sleep well?"

Max jumped up. "Hi, Wilbur, where've you been?"

"I was next to you the whole time. We guardian angels are always there, even when you don't see us."

"Why did you turn invisible again?"

"Because when we're invisible, we never get tired, and we can fly much faster."

"How fast?"

"Faster than you can think."

Max thought about that. Faster than he could think. Wow, that had to be pretty fast!

"Time to get up, Max! Breakfast is ready," Mother called from the kitchen.

Max slid into his slippers. "Come on, Wilbur, let's eat!"

Wilbur could smell the hot chocolate even before he got into the kitchen. And before Max could say a thing, he heard a loud splash! A chocolate fountain sprayed over the table. Max stared at Wilbur who was practically drowning in the hot chocolate. "What is that?" screeched Max's mother.

Max scooped Wilbur out of the cup and put him on the
table. "May I introduce you? This is Wilbur, my guardian
angel," he said.
Wilbur looked like a chocolate angel. Max giggled. Wilbur
wasn't amused. The more Max giggled, the more Wilbur
pouted.
Mother had recovered a bit from her shock. Curiously, she
stared at Wilbur.

"Sticky angels are dangerous," Mother declared.
Max didn't know how she knew that.
"Straight to the bath, both of you," she shouted.
Clean as a whistle, Wilbur got out of the bath and did a trial flight,
complete with aerobatic loops. Max applauded, spraying water all
over the bathroom. When he got out of the tub, he said, "I wish I
could fly too!"

Wilbur landed on the sink. "You want to fly? I could teach you, if you want."

"You could? Now?" Max was so excited.

"No. I have to train you in the art of dreamflying first. And you must be asleep in order to do that."

"How about tonight?"

"Maybe."

Max could hardly wait!

For the next few days, practically all they talked about was flying. Wilbur kept himself busy by eating huge quantities of chocolate and thinking of new ways to give Max's mother a fright. And every night, Max asked Wilbur: "Is tonight the night?"

Finally, it was time. While Max slept, Wilbur snuck into his dreams, and taught him how to fly. First just a short flight, then as high as the pear tree. Max was a quick learner, and soon they flew in Max's dreams all the way to the end of the earth.

Flying was more beautiful than anything Max had ever imagined. It tickled in his tummy. When he was flying with Wilbur, he forgot about being the new boy in town and wasn't lonely or bored at all. Effortlessly, Max and Wilbur soared through the air, high up over the clouds. Sometimes they soared low, over forests filled with unusual animals. Sometimes they flew fast, and other times just floated along slowly.

But one night, just as Max was trying to fly especially high, he heard Wilbur calling. "Max! Wait! I can't fly so high!"

Max flew back, and saw that Wilbur could barely keep himself airborne.

"You've eaten too much chocolate," said Max. "You've become so fat that your wings can hardly carry you anymore."

Wilbur was completely out of breath. Luckily, they weren't far from home. Max could see his window.

"Wilbur, I'm worried that if you don't stop eating so much chocolate, it won't be long before you're too heavy to fly at all."

"I know. But when I'm visible, I just can't resist chocolate. It's only when I'm invisible that I don't feel like eating it."

"Then you should make yourself invisible," said Max. "You've been great, Wilbur. You really cheered me up, and I thank you. But you have to be able to fly!"

In less time than it takes to blink your eye, Wilbur disappeared from sight.

"Hey, Wilbur?"

"Don't shout, I'm right next to you."

"I can't see you," said Max anxiously.

"But I can see you. True as my name is Wilbur. I can even see you in the dark. Watch that you don't fly into any walls!" Wilbur giggled.

Then all was quiet.

That was the last time that Max
saw Wilbur. At first he was sad, but
then he got used to it. He knew
that there were guardian angels,
and that his was always close by.
Occasionally he would talk to his
mother about Wilbur. And every
now and then he would fly in his
dreams—but by himself.

Sometimes Max could feel just the
tiniest puff of wind in his room—
like the flutter of little wings.
Then he would smile and eat a
piece of chocolate.